Charlie's Great Adventures #2

Charlie
Moves to Arizona

by

C.A. GOODY

To Amber,
Annastasia, +
Wesley;
Love + blessings,
C.A. Goody

illustrated by

TERRY LAAKER

Cover design by Reid Johns and Rich Highland
Written and Printed in the U.S.A.
Typeset and Printed by TKPrinting

Copyright (c) 2001 by C.A. Goody

First Printing November 2001
ISBN 0-9702546-9-5

Goody, C.A. 1962-
Charlie Moves to Arizona, C.A. Goody

Summary - Charlie the cat and his family move to Arizona where he must adapt to life in the desert.

1 -Animal Adventure   2 - Cats   3 - Humor   4 - Childrens

DEDICATIONS

To My Lord Jesus Christ,
who makes all things possible.

And to Edward; my partner, my hero, my love;
who supports me and puts up with me,
no matter what.

Make sure to read all of
Charlie's Great Adventures:

**Charlie's Great Adventure
Charlie Moves to Arizona**

Coming in 2002

Charlie and the Rodent Queen

For more information on *Charlie*,
check out our web site at:

www.charliethecat.com

TABLE OF CONTENTS

Chapter 1

I was a Happy Cat

HELLO, MY NAME IS CHARLIE. I'm a cat. Technically, I'm an abyssinian cat, but that's just my breed. The only really good thing about being a pure-bred, for me, is that I look like a cougar but with a tabby cat's face. I'm the size of a house cat, of course.

I was born on a farm in Northern California and adopted by a great family that moved me to the city. My special person is a little girl named Amanda. She has long blonde hair and blue eyes and she loves to spin me in circles and hug me. She has a little brother named Andrew. We were both babies when I moved in with the family, but somehow I grew up and he didn't. I'm one year old now (in people years) and Andrew is two, but I guess people don't grow up as fast as cats do. Not that he isn't bigger than I am. Even though he's the baby of the family, he could still play giant and crush me with one foot if he wanted to. Luckily he's a nice kid, and I can run fast. I also like the way he talks. When I first moved in he just made funny noises that sounded more like 'meows' than people words. Now he can actually say words, but it still sounds like some strange, half-cat language.

There are two other people in our family. First is Mom. She's the nice lady who feeds us all and gives us hugs. Then there's Dad. He goes to work every-day, and sometimes he goes on trips for a few days at a time. I don't like it when he's gone too long, be-cause Dad's the one who always brings out the flash-light for me to play with. When he pulls that thing out, this little circle of light appears, and I can chase it all over the room. Even up the walls. Besides, ev-eryone is happier when the whole family is together.

We do have one other member of our family. The dog. Her name is Frisky and, to put it nicely, she's not too bright. She is big and brown and likes to lick me all over. Yuck. But I figured out from the begin-ning that as long as I don't mess with her food, I can out-think her enough to make up for our size differ-ence. We made an agreement when I first moved in that if she would be careful not to step on me, I would keep all my claws inside my paws when she's around.

We all live in a cozy house with just enough room for all of us (as long as they leave Frisky outside). I stay inside most of the time, but I go out in the back-yard for a little while each day to lay in the sun and play 'Tiger in the Grass' and 'Big Game Hunter'. I never go in the front yard anymore, since the one time I did, I got chased by a bully and was lost for several days. But that's another story.

One of my favorite things to do is bug hunting. We live in a very clean neighborhood, so there are no mice around anywhere (which is probably a good thing because the idea of eating a mouse really grosses me out). Needing to pounce as much as any cat, I learned at a very young age to hunt bugs. Grasshoppers are great because they are hard to catch, but if they spit in your face before you eat them, it ruins the flavor. Beetles are too easy to catch, no challenge involved, but they have a nice crunchy taste that I really like. Potato Bugs are very simple to get a hold of, but they roll themselves into a little ball and can get stuck in your throat. There's nothing worse than choking on a bug.

A typical day for me starts when the alarm goes off in Amanda's room. I sleep on her bed at night and stretch when the music starts playing early in the morning. Dad leaves the house when it's still dark, and sometimes I'll get up for a few minutes to say good-bye to him, but I go back to bed after he leaves until Amanda is ready to rise and shine.

So I lay there in bed and watch Amanda wake up. Usually the music plays for a little while, then she turns it off and goes back to sleep until Mom comes in and says she'll be late for school if she doesn't get up. Then she stretches, reaches over to pet me a couple times, and gets up to get dressed. I slowly stretch. I have no place important to go until I actually hear Mom in the kitchen making breakfast. Then I race down the hall to be the first served. I rub up against Mom's legs, meowing softly to let her know I'm ready, even if no one else is yet. She says something nice like, "Good morning Charlie," and gives me a nice bowl of warm milk.

Then Andrew comes in for his breakfast. Mom has two tables in the kitchen, one for the family and one just for the kids. The kid table looks like a miniature picnic bench, and I have to duck to go under the seats on either side. Andrew sits down at the little table to eat and I climb under there to clean up any mess he leaves. And believe me, there's usually some good stuff to clean up.

Amanda rushes in last and always takes at least ten minutes to decide what she wants to eat. The choices are almost always the same, but she still makes Mom repeat each possible breakfast at least three times before she will commit to one.

"Cereal, toast, eggs, oatmeal or yogurt," Mom says.

"What was the third thing?" Amanda will ask.

"Eggs."

"Can you say them all again, slower this time."

"Cereal...toast...eggs...oatmeal...yogurt." Mom's starting to look irate.

"Umm, well, I don't know..."

"Okay, cereal it is," Mom decides.

"No! Yogurt and a banana," Amanda answers. It's the same every morning.

After everybody has eaten and gotten ready, Mom drives Amanda to school. Then I goof around while Andrew and Mom play games and sing or clean the house. When Andrew goes for his nap after lunch, Mom and I watch TV together and snack. Actually, Mom pets me while she watches TV and I sneak some of her lunch.

Not long after nap time Amanda comes home and we all have a snack and play for awhile. I go into the backyard and chase bugs while Amanda and Andrew swing. Sometimes they try to take me on the swing with them, but I don't let them do that very often. All that up and down, up and down can really make you dizzy. We cats prefer to keep our feet firmly planted on the ground, thank you very much.

Dad comes home in the afternoon and plays 'roughhouse' with Amanda and Andrew. They all roll around on the floor together in a big ball and wrestle. I made the mistake of trying to join in on that game once, but my only defense is my teeth and claws, and Dad says that's cheating. Let him wrestle a giant and see if he doesn't use his teeth. Humph.

Dinner is eaten all together at the big table. When I say all together, I mean the people sit in the chairs and I sit under the table, in the hope that Mom has made something the kids don't like. Liver for example. When liver is on the menu more pieces of food are 'accidentally' dropped to the floor than on any other night. Frisky gets to come inside after dinner to clean up anything I miss, but she doesn't even know that liver exists, because there's never any left by the time she gets to the table. On the other hand, I never get any food on hot dog night, because Amanda and Andrew eat every bite.

After dinner the rest of the family usually takes Frisky for a walk. I relax and catch a cat nap so I can stay up late. When they get home the kids take a bath, get ready for bed, then listen to Mom read a story. That's a fun time of the day. Everybody, even Dad and I, cuddle up together on the couch and imagine whatever adventure Mom is reading to us. Sometimes the stories get a little scary and we all snuggle really close, and other times they're so funny that Mom has to stop reading until we finish laughing. Amanda likes mysteries best, Andrew likes anything funny and I like the animal stories. Especially the ones about cats. If the story is about a dog, I always find myself cheering on the dog catcher.

Then the kids go to bed. Dad and Mom sit down together and talk quietly about what they did all day. Sometimes they watch TV and I sit on both of their laps at the same time while they pet me.

It's a great life.

At least, it was a great life. Until the day Dad came home and said we were moving.

Chapter 2

The Bad News.....

IT WAS JUST AN ORDINARY DAY. I had been out-side chasing bugs (I had actually managed to snag a moth right out of the air!). The kids were playing out back and I was resting on the sofa, when I heard Dad come through the front door. He sounded really excited as he talked to Mom, and when I looked into the kitchen, I could see them smiling and hugging each other. But that wasn't unusual. Mom and Dad hugged every-body, all the time. I just figured Dad had a good day.

They told us at dinner. Not that I really un-derstood at that time what it all meant.

Dad started out by saying, "Do you kids re-member when we went to visit my friends in Arizona last spring?"

"Yeah, and we got to ride on the airplane!" Amanda answered.

"And saw wizards!" said Andrew in his cute little baby voice.

"Lizards? Oh yeah, there were lizards climbing on the back fence at their house. Good memory Andrew," Dad said.

"Me smart," Andrew beamed a huge smile around the table.

"Anyway," Dad began again, "I've been offered a new job down there. It's really a great opportunity for me, and I think for all of us. Mom and I have been talking about it for a while and we think it would be a good idea to move there. We'll be able to get a nice new house in a great neighborhood with lots of other kids, and the schools are really good. Mom will be able to stay home with you full time and not have to worry so much about money. What do you guys think?"

What do they think? I don't care what they think, I don't want to move!

"What about Grandma and Grandpa?" Amanda asked. "I'll miss them if we move away."

"We talked about that too, honey," Mom said. "Your grandparents will be able to come down to visit us. We won't see them as much as we do now, but we will see them."

"And I promise we can come back here for Christmas every year, so that we can spend the holidays with the entire family," Dad added.

"Doesn't it get really hot there?" Amanda asked.

"It does in the summer, but we'll have a pool and air conditioning, so it won't be that bad. And the winter there is great. It doesn't get very cold, and practically never rains, so you can play outside almost every day." Dad was really starting to hard sell this idea.

"What 'bout my swing-set?" Andrew wanted to know. "We gonna move dat?"

"No, but we'll get you a brand new one, even bigger and better," Mom said. I guess she really wanted to sell this move too.

"What about all our toys? Do we have to leave those here?" Amanda asked with real concern.

"No, no honey. We'll take all of our stuff with us. All your furniture and toys and clothes. Our new house will be different, but all your things will be the same," Dad reassured her.

"What we going do wiff dis house?" Andrew wanted to know.

"We'll put it up for sale. Someone else will buy this house and we will buy a new one," Mom said.

"This is a very nice house," Amanda said sadly. "The people who buy it will be very lucky."

"I agree sweetheart," Mom said. "I like this house a lot too, and it makes me a little sad to think about leaving it. But then I think about getting a brand new house, bigger and full of sunshine and near a really good school. That makes me very happy."

"Okay Daddy," Amanda said. "When do we move?"

"As soon as we sell the house here. We have to get the money from selling this house to get the new one," Dad answered.

Andrew shook his head in approval and I knew the discussion was over. They started talking about how long it would take to sell the house and what things were going to be like for the next few weeks, but I had stopped listening. I couldn't believe what was happening. How could they have made this kind of major decision without asking me? I had no desire to move. I liked things just as they were, thank you very much.

I walked toward the back door, shaking my head. The door was open so I called to Frisky through the screen. "Hey Frisky, I need to talk to you. You won't believe what's happened."

Frisky ran to the door and cocked her head to one side. "What is it Charlie?" she asked in her dizzy little voice.

"Dad just announced that we're going to sell the house and move to another state. Can you believe it? I just can't understand why they're doing this to us."

"Oh, did they finally decide? It's okay Charlie. We'll be getting a big new house with a bigger backyard with more room to run in."

"What?" I asked incredulously. "You knew they were thinking about this?"

"Of course. Dad's been telling me about it for weeks. Everytime he got ready to leave on one of his trips, he would tell me he was sorry he wouldn't see me for a few days and he would explain to me everything he was trying to do. You see, he's going to be starting this new business, and...."

"Stop!" I yelled. "I don't believe this! You knew this for weeks and didn't bother to tell me about it?"

"I figured you already knew," that dingy voice rang in my ears. "After all, you're inside a lot more of the time than I am. Didn't Mom say anything to you?"

Had she? I thought about it. Sometimes at night when Dad was gone, Mom would sit on the couch and pet me and talk about things. But lately I had been enjoying the petting so much that I hadn't been paying much attention to what she said. Maybe she had told me and I just hadn't been listening. Maybe I just hadn't wanted to hear.

But that still didn't change the situation. "Aren't you upset about moving?" I asked Frisky.

"Should I be?" she cocked her head to one side again, as if the information she was looking for in her brain might slide into place that way.

"Of course you should be!" Sometimes I just couldn't believe how slow this dog was. "We'll be leaving everything we know behind. All our special hiding places, all the familiar smells, even your dog friends that you bark to all the time. Doesn't that make you sad?"

"Well, yeah, I guess that will make me sad," she said. "But our family will be there Charlie. And home is wherever our family is."

I stared at her. She was right. I was worried about unimportant things when all that really mattered was being a part of the family. Maybe I had underestimated Frisky. Maybe she wasn't as dumb as I thought she was.

Nah.

But maybe it wasn't too late. Dad said we couldn't move until they sold the house. If I could just think of a way to keep it from selling...

Chapter 3

How To Gross Out House Hunters

THE NEXT DAY DAD PHONED THIS PERSON called a Realtor. He came over and walked through the house and said how nice it was and then told us everything that was wrong with it. When he left he put a big sign out on the front lawn. I watched through the window as he pounded it in. It said "FOR SALE" in bold letters. Every swing of the hammer seemed like an arm waving good-bye.

Mom became a whirlwind. She was constantly cleaning the house now. Every time somebody dropped anything on the floor, Mom was there to pick it up. Beds were made in the morning almost before we got out of them. The kitchen was so clean Dad said we could eat off the floor. I thought that was a strange thing to say, since I always ate off the floor.

Amanda and Andrew nearly went crazy during that time. Mom was picking up their toys faster than they could play with them. If they left a toy for a few minutes to go check on something in another room, the toy would be gone when they came back. I learned something interesting then. Human children don't like things clean. They like having all their toys out in the open where they can see them and be sure nothing is missing and no one else is playing with them. So Amanda and Andrew would pull all the toys out of their cabinets and closets and put them on the floor. Mom would come in, say the room was a mess and to clean up everything except what they were actually playing with. So it became an adventure to try to play with as many toys at one time as they could, so they would have an excuse for not picking them up.

It didn't take too long for Mom to calm down and only insist on a full clean up when someone had called and said they were coming over to look at the house. Then she would take out one set of toys for the kids to play with while the people were there.

I hated when the people came. They would walk through the house, talking in hushed voices about what they liked and didn't like about the place. Every time someone came in I would try to picture them living in the house instead of us. But I couldn't. None of them

22

were good enough for our house. None of them seemed to me to be as happy and nice as my family, so they didn't deserve to live in our house. It was a warm, friendly place, and only really good people should live there. So I came up with a few ideas to keep anyone from buying it.

Whenever the phone rang and Mom started cleaning right away, I knew someone was coming to look at the house. Then I would spring into action. The first trick I came up with was the bugs. No matter how much Mom cleaned, I knew if people found bugs all around they would think there was a problem with the house. So I would save all the bugs I hunted for days at a time. This was a deep, personal sacrifice for me, since bugs were my favorite snack, but it was worth it. When I knew someone was coming over, I would gather up several of my bugs and place them all over the front walk and porch. As people walked up to the front door they would hear a funny crunch, look down, and see that they were stepping on dead bugs. That would usually freak them out enough that they really didn't notice the rest of the house.

My second trick was sneakier and stinkier. While I was in the backyard gathering bugs to put on the front porch when people were coming over, I would eat some of Frisky's dog food. It tasted awful, and it always gave me terrible gas. But that was the idea.

After distributing the bugs out front, I would go to the living room and clear all the gas out of my system. But I never burped, if you know what I mean. By the time the potential buyers got there and walked to the living room, I had created a gross enough smell that they got out of the house fast. They never knew that the smell was only temporary.

It took quite a while for anyone to catch on and figure out what I was up to. The family would either leave the house or get out of the way when it was being shown, so they never knew why people wanted out of there so fast. I think it was the Realtor who finally figured it out and advised Mom to send me outside when people were coming over. So I was banished from the house during showings.

But that didn't stop me. No way.

I found a new target. The Realtor had something called an "Open House". This was a day where anyone could just walk into the house all day long and look around without having to make an appointment. It was a great opportunity for me.

I hid in the bushes as soon as the Realtor got there. Dad and Mom took the kids out for the day so they wouldn't be in the way. The Realtor was the only one there, showing people through. He must have wondered why no one came in all day. He was there for over eight hours and didn't show the house once. Little did he know that everytime someone walked up to the front door, before they could climb the steps and ring the bell, I would pounce on their ankles and chase them away. That was one fun day!

And the cleaning continued.

Finally, on a day when Dad was actually home and playing with us, Mom came into the room all excited after talking on the phone. They had sold the house. Everything was set, all they had to do was sign the papers.

I had no idea who had bought the place, but they either came to look at the house when I wasn't aware of it, or they liked dirty, smelly houses.

I walked up to Mom and meowed softly. She picked me up and looked at me, and I could see she was trying to figure out what I wanted.

"Meow," I said softly. Are you sure this is what we have to do?

"It's okay, Charlie," she said. "Our new home will be a great place for you, too. I know you're probably a little confused with everything that's been going on, but I'm sure you'll be happy once we get settled again." She stroked me under the chin a few times. "Better now?"

"Meow," I answered. I always answered when Mom talked to me. And this time I really did feel better. Maybe this wouldn't be so bad after all. Maybe I really would like our new home even better.

Maybe.

Chapter 4

Adventures in a Moving Van

THINGS MOVED PRETTY QUICKLY AFTER THAT. One day a huge truck pulled up in front of the house and parked. Dad said it was the moving van that would take all our stuff to our new home.

Mom started packing everything into boxes. All the dishes, toys, clothes, everything. You name it, it went in a box. Then Dad took the boxes and loaded them into the truck.

Uncle Glenn came over to help. Uncle Glenn is a big man with big hands and a great big smile. He always likes to pick up Amanda and swing her around in circles in the air, the same way Amanda swings me around. The first time I saw him do that I was really afraid Amanda would go flying out one of the windows. After all, she doesn't have claws to hold on with like I do.

Uncle Glenn is a nice enough guy. He always says "Hi Charlie," to me and pets me when he comes over, unlike some people who chose to ignore animals. But there is one big problem with Uncle Glenn. Actually two big ones and a small one. His dogs.

He always had at least one of them with him when he came over. If he brought his dog Penny, it was no big deal. Penny was a miniature something or another and was a little smaller than I was. She liked to think she was tough and would run up and bark at me. Yeah, right. Like I'm going to take that from some little pooch. I just had to show her my claws and let out a loud hiss, and she would be hiding under the sofa for the rest of her visit. I actually kind of liked her.

But then there were the other two. I never got their names, I never stayed around long enough to find them out. They were German Shepherds. Big German Shepherds. I mean BIG German Shepherds. Those two dogs would have eaten me in one bite and called me an appetizer if I ever gave them the chance. Whenever they came in the door I would run to Mom and Dad's bedroom and hide behind the bed until they left.

The one time I did stay and watch them was the time Uncle Glenn brought all three dogs on the same day. They didn't come in the house, but stayed out front with Uncle Glenn and Dad. You want to know something really funny? Penny was the boss. Really, I mean it! This tiny dog, smaller than most cats, was standing there telling these great big German Shepherds what to do. And they did it! Imagine a grumpy little old lady telling two big football players how to play the game better, and you've got the picture. I sat in the window and laughed my head off watching them. When they spotted me the big dogs started to growl, but when Penny told them to stop it, they did! The next time Penny came over, I shared my rubber mouse with her.

On the day we were packing to move, Uncle Glenn didn't bring any of the dogs. I guess he figured they would just be in the way. Frisky certainly was. Every time Dad tried to carry a box through the house, Frisky would jump right in front of him to check out what it was and end up almost tripping Dad. Me, I knew how to stay out of the way and actually be of help. I would jump up while Mom was packing the boxes, get inside the box and check to make sure she had everything secured correctly.

Unfortunately, Mom didn't seem to appreciate my help and kept telling me to get out of the boxes and to stay out of the way. I continued to try to help, and you know what she did? She threw me out back! She put Frisky out too, but Frisky deserved it. I was only attempting to be useful.

Once I was in the back yard, I decided to check out the moving van. After all, it had been parked out front all morning, and it was open since Dad and Uncle Glenn were constantly loading boxes and furniture in. I'd never been in the back of a big truck before. The only other time I had been in the back of a truck, I had found a tuna fish sandwich inside. And I LOVE tuna. Maybe a bigger truck would have bigger sandwiches? It was worth checking out.

I jumped over the fence and walked slowly around to the front of the house. I sniffed the air and the ground carefully to make sure there were no other animals around. I knew a large, mean cat lived next door, and I never wanted to meet up with him again. When I reached the front bushes I hid behind them until Dad and Uncle Glenn left the truck. I wanted to explore on my own, so I waited until they went into the house. Then I snuck up to the tailgate.

The inside of the truck was huge. It looked even larger than it had from outside. Dad already had tons of boxes and furniture stacked neatly against the back and side walls. It looked like a gigantic mountain. And since I like to pretend I'm a mountain lion, I decided to go for a climb.

I picked my way very carefully to the top. The inside of the truck had an interesting blend of smells.

Smells from every room of our house, all mixed together, plus a weird mix of other smells that must have been from other people who had used the truck before. I climbed up to the top at the very back, where it connected to the cab. There was a small ironing board sitting on top of one of the boxes. It reminded me of a flat rock like a mountain lion would lay on, so I stepped onto it, pretending to bask in the sunshine.

Big mistake. Somehow I must have leaned a little too far to one side while I was pretending to bask, and the ironing board began to fall. It started sliding down the mountain of boxes and furniture, slowly at first, then gaining speed. At first I was really scared, but then I realized it was kind of like surfing. So I hung on with all twenty claws and let out an excited yell. "Cat-a-bunga!"

Boxes were falling to the ground behind me as I continued to surf down the mound, and it made the adventure even more exciting as I imagined they were waves crashing all around. I was having the time of my life until I reached the bottom. As the last of the boxes collapsed behind me, I leaped forward, very pleased with myself that I had escaped the great adventure unharmed.

That's when I saw Dad looking at me from the tailgate.

I spent the rest of the day locked in the bathroom with nothing but my litter box and some cat food. They didn't let me out until it was time to leave.

It was really weird walking out of that bathroom. The house was empty. I mean completely empty. No furniture, no pictures, no toys, no clothes, nothing. Just empty rooms that echoed as you walked through them.

Amanda carried me to the door and stopped. She looked kind of sad as she glanced back into the barren rooms. She said softly "Good-bye house."

I looked back and meowed a soft good-bye. This was the only house I had ever lived in.

But the minute we walked out the door, a new excitement seemed to come over both of us. We were on our way to a new place, a new home, a new life. We looked forward toward a bright new future.

I looked forward and saw the car. It was then that it dawned on me that we were going to have to drive to this new future.

Chapter 5

Station Wagon...or Torture Chamber?

AMANDA CARRIED ME TO THE STATION WAGON and climbed in. Dad was riding in the moving truck with the driver and Mom was driving the car with Amanda, Andrew and I in the back seat. Frisky sat all the way in the very back.

I guess I haven't mentioned up until now how much I hate to ride in the car. I don't really know why I hate it so much, but I do. Every time I have to go in the car I cry and scream and try to get out the windows. It's just the way I am. I feel like I'm trapped and have no control.

So you can imagine my reaction when we got into the car and I heard Amanda ask, "How long until we get to our new home Mom?" and Mom answered,

"About fourteen hours."

Fourteen hours? In the car? No way!

I started meowing really loud and pawing at the windows. I had changed my mind. I wasn't going. Just leave me here and I'll see if the new family will keep me. I love you all, but I am NOT going to be in a car for that length of time.

Do you know what they did to me? Instead of letting me out of the car, they put me in a cat carrier! A cat carrier is a very small cage with tiny windows that just barely let in enough air. At least, that's how mine felt. All I did, once they put me inside, was to howl even louder.

Frisky was having problems of her own. Somehow she had gotten confused about what was going on (not that it takes much to confuse her), and she started whimpering. I don't know if she had changed her mind and didn't want to leave, or if she was sad about moving, or if she wanted to be riding in the big truck with Dad. I never did figure out what her problem was. All I know is that she whined the whole trip.

So imagine this if you can; the kids playing and fighting and yelling, Mom trying to drive and keep the kids in line, Frisky whining and me yowling. This went on for the entire drive. Not a pretty picture, is it?

We did stop occasionally. Every two or three hours we would stop and everybody would get out of the car. Everybody that is, except me. Apparently they thought I might bolt away from the car and never come back. And believe me, I considered it. I knew being lost and alone was no fun, but I figured anything was better than being in that car.

When everyone got out of the car, Mom would let me out of my carrier, set out a litter box and some cat food, then leave. I watched them all through the windows. A lot of the stops were at places called "Rest Areas." On those stops everybody would go into the bathrooms, then run around on the grass for awhile to stretch their legs. Even Frisky got to get out and run. I stood on the dashboard of the station wagon, howling my head off for someone to let me out.

Some of the stops were at fast-food places. Frisky had to stay in the car at those stops, but she didn't mind because Mom always brought back a hamburger for her.

Mom would bring some meat for me too, but I didn't eat it. In fact, I didn't eat or drink anything the entire trip. I was too upset. You might even say I went a little bonkers that day, but I prefer to think of it as a slight storm in my normally sunny disposition. Well, maybe more like a hurricane.

The kids cheered when we crossed the border into Arizona, and they got very excited when they started seeing cactus on the side of the road just a few minutes later. I didn't know what cactus were yet, and I didn't particularly care. Mom said there was still at least two hours of driving ahead of us, and I already felt like I had spent half my life in that car.

Finally, after what seemed like an eternity, we stopped in front of a house. "This is it," Mom said. "Our new home."

It was a nice looking house from the outside. It was white, with a red tile roof. There was nice green grass in the front yard, and some bushes with beautiful red flowers on them. Suddenly I was excited again. I couldn't wait to explore my new home.

And what was the first thing they did with me? They took me out of the box, carried me inside, and locked me in the bathroom with a litter box and some cat food.

Chapter 6

The Haunted House

THEY DIDN'T LET ME OUT until all the furniture had been moved into the house. It was very strange walking through that house for the first time. Everything was new, yet all our old things were there, so it felt somehow familiar.

It was bigger than our old house. The walls were all painted white, and they looked naked because there were no pictures hung on them yet. The carpet was great. It was a color somewhere between brown and white, and it was thick and soft. My paws just sank down into all that fluff.

I walked by Andrew's room and saw him unpacking all his toys from big boxes. It looked like he would be busy unpacking for several days, since he had to play with each toy as he took it out of the box.

Farther down the hall was Amanda's room. She was

also busy unpacking, and I went in to explore, since this would be the room where I would be sleeping too. It was a little smaller than her old room, and she was having some trouble trying to figure out where to put all her dolls and books. I decided to help by playing a game.

Amanda hadn't noticed me come into the room. She was sitting facing the bed, with a big box next to her and a pile of small dolls and all their stuff in front of her. I carefully slipped under the bed. Then, as she turned her head to get something out of the box, I reached out a paw and grabbed one of the dolls and pulled it under the bed with me. I carried the doll all the way over to the middle of the bed, then went back over to the side where Amanda was.

She hadn't noticed the doll was missing, so when she turned back to the box again, I snuck another doll. I kept on doing this for several minutes, snagging a couch, a sink, three dresses and eight shoes along with about twelve dolls.

Finally, when the box was empty, Amanda turned around and noticed that the pile looked a little small. She glanced around the room, looking for the missing things. That's when I made my mistake. While she had her head turned, I tried to take one more dress, and she turned just in time to see it disappear under the bed.

She just stared at first, unsure how the dress was moving under the bed all by itself. Then she started screaming. "MOMMY!"

Mom came running into the bedroom. "What's the matter honey?"

"This house is haunted! My doll clothes are disappearing under the bed all by themselves! I saw one moving! There are ghosts here!!!"

"Calm down honey. I'm sure there's a logical explanation. This house is much too new for a ghost to live here, and we don't even believe in ghosts. Now, let's have a look." Mom bent down to look under the bed and Amanda looked under with her. I was hidden behind the big pile of dolls, clothes and furniture, so they couldn't see me.

"See Mom, all that stuff went under there by itself!" Amanda cried.

Mom looked very closely at the pile. "Amanda, do you have a real fur stole for your dolls?"

"No, I don't have anything made out of real fur," Amanda answered.

"Then I have found the answer to our mystery, because there is a tail in the middle of the pile."

Amanda looked puzzled for a moment, then let out a yell. "CHARLIE!" She looked a little mad to begin with, but Mom was losing her battle not to laugh and pretty soon Amanda joined in.

"No more worries about ghosts, okay?" Mom asked. "You just have an overactive imagination and an overactive cat."

As Amanda started pulling all the stuff I had piled up out from under the bed, I decided it was time to check out the yard. I went to the back door and meowed until Dad let me out.

I loved it. The yard was big, with green grass all around two sides of the house and a tall metal circle on the other side. There were bushes all around the fences with beautiful pink, yellow, purple and red flowers. The sun was shining brightly, and when I stepped out into that sunshine it warmed my fur clear through. All cats love napping in the sun, especially in the winter, and I got that same 'warm all over' feeling just standing there.

I started walking around the back yard, and next thing I knew, I was dancing. It was just so pretty and warm and happy feeling that I couldn't help myself. Frisky was sleeping on a corner of the lawn when I came out. I think she thought I was nuts at first, skipping around the back yard with my tail flying high, but as she stepped out into the sun, she started dancing too. She looked so foolish jumping around and swinging her tail that I realized how silly I must look.

I stopped immediately. One thing about cats, we try to maintain our dignity. It's not always easy when we get caught doing something like chasing our own tails, but we try. So I straightened myself up, looked around to make sure nobody but Frisky had seen me acting so crazy, and walked over to look at the flowers by the fence.

Frisky was still dancing, and I was just starting to get a good whiff of the roses when I heard a voice over my head. "Welcome to the neighborhood."

I looked up to see a black cat sitting above me on top of the fence. I took a step back to make sure he wasn't going to pounce on me, but when I realized he wasn't making any threatening moves I calmed back down. "Thank you," I answered. "My name is Charlie. What's yours?"

"Blackie's the name. You and your family just moved in today, right?" I nodded. "Where you all from?"

"Northern California. It's a long car ride from here, I can tell you that. How long have you lived here?" I asked.

"Three long years," he said with a sigh. His voice was deep and kind of raspy, like an old jazz singer. "We moved here from New York. The city and the state. It was a huge change moving from the big city to this backwater desert, let me tell you. Are you from the city Charlie?" Blackie asked with interest.

"Well, it was a city, but not a big city like New York." I had seen pictures of New York City in books and on TV. I had been lost in a city once, and didn't care for them too much, but New York looked exciting. It would be fun to learn more about it from my new friend.

"Hey Charlie, is the mutt cool?" Blackie asked.

"What?"

"The mutt. You know, the dog over there, dancing around the yard. She looks like she's crazy, but does she like cats?"

I looked over at Frisky. She was still dancing around, in circles now, and to the tune of the birds in the tree out front. She looked really silly, and I was glad I had stopped dancing before Blackie had gotten there.

"Well, Frisky's okay with me, but I don't know if she would allow any other cats in the yard. She's kind of protective about her space, and only shares it with me because I'm family," I answered.

"You call that dog 'family'? That's pretty brave. Most cats I know won't even go near a dog, let alone admit to living with one." Blackie looked at me like he was trying to figure out what kind of a cat I really was.

"Well, I didn't have much choice in the matter," I admitted. "Frisky was living with the family when I moved in, so she's just part of the package.

"Besides, we have an understanding. She pretty much leaves me alone." I didn't want to admit that Frisky and I were actually pretty close friends. I didn't know Blackie very well yet, and some cats really look down on you for associating with dogs.

"I have a dog in my family too," Blackie said. "Ralph and I are really very tight."

"What do you mean, tight?" I asked.

"You know, we like each other. I know that's a crazy thing to say about a dog and a cat, but we've been living together for so many years that I can't help but feel kind of attached to the mutt. He was just a pup when he came to live with my family, and I brought him up right. He don't bother me or any lady cat I might bring home with me, but he chases any uninvited guests over the fence faster that you can say Jack Robinson."

"Who's Jack Robinson?" I asked.

"Oh Charlie," Blackie laughed, "you really are young, aren't you? That's just an old expression. Never mind. What do you think of the desert so far?"

"It's fabulous! It's the middle of the winter and it's so warm and sunny. Is it sunny all the time here?"

"Almost all the time," Blackie said. "In the winter it's great, but you won't appreciate that sun nearly as much once summer comes, let me tell you!"

I wasn't quite sure what that meant, so I decided to change the subject. "Everything here is so different from my old home. Even the plants look strange. What's that pretty one over there called? It's so big and delicate looking!" As I asked the question I was walking toward this tall green plant with two huge yellow flowers growing out of the top.

"Charlie, I wouldn't try to sniff that one if I were you!" Blackie said. But his warning came too late. I had already put my paw up on the plant to get my nose near the flower.

"OWOWOWOWOW!" My paw had a hole in it! As I started licking the blood off, I looked more closely at the strange green plant that had bitten me. It had short thorns sticking out all over.

Blackie was trying hard not to laugh. "Ah, Charlie? Haven't you ever seen a cactus before?"

"No, what's a cactus?"

"That plant you just touched. That's one kind of cacti. There are a lot of other kinds, all over around here. So always look closely at a plant before you touch it. In fact, you should be careful even smelling them. Some of them can actually shoot their thorns at you if they think you're going to hurt them."

My eyes must have bulged out of my head. "You mean the plants here can think?" I asked in amazement.

"Well, not like you and me. They don't really have brains, but they can kind of sense danger. You better be a little more careful Charlie. The desert can be a beautiful and magical place. It can also be very dangerous. There are animals and plants here that you won't find anywhere else, so you don't know how to deal with them yet. If you run into anything you don't understand, just give me a holler and I'll see if I can help out."

"I really appreciate that. It looks like I have a lot to learn." I was quiet for a moment, licking my sore paw, wondering if I would be able to adjust to this new place. I decided to change the subject again. "So, what does a cat do for fun around here?"

"Well now, that depends," Blackie looked at me

questioningly. "Do you like music?"

"I love it! Next to my family, it's one of my very favorite things!"

"Well, we've got a little night club down the street here. Me and some of the other cats got ourselves a little band, and we entertain for the neighborhood. Maybe you'd like to check it out sometime. What kind of music are you into, Charlie?"

"I was raised on classical music, but I've also listened to a lot of rock and pop with my family," I answered.

"Well, we play jazz, so I don't know what you'll think of us. Anyway, I better go for now, it's almost suppertime for me." He turned around, and as he jumped down the other side of the fence I heard him yell, "see ya later, Charlie!"

After Blackie disappeared over his side of the fence, I started to wonder who might live on the other side of the house. I jumped up on the garbage can by the wall and from there leaped on top of the fence. I walked to the far side of the yard and looked over at the neighbors place. There, sitting on a covered patio, was a strange looking creature.

It was larger than a kitten, but smaller than me. It had HUGE ears, a long skinny tail like a rat, and almost no fur. It was looking at the back door of it's house and shivering. That didn't make much sense either. It was very warm, so why was it shivering? Then it turned to look at me. It had great big round black eyes. It blinked twice, but didn't say anything.

Normally I'm very polite, but I was so mystified by this weird animal that I forgot my manners. I heard myself say, "What are you?"

"What 'chou mean?" a male voice with a heavy Hispanic accent came out of its tiny little mouth.

"What - kind - of - a - creature - are - you?" I asked very slowly, in case he hadn't understood my English.

"I'm a dog man," he answered in a tone that said I had asked a really stupid question.

I laughed. "No, really, what are you?"

"I am a Chihuahua. A small hairless dog from Mexico." I started laughing harder. "Don't laugh at me man. You're not so big yourself, you know. You look like a lion who got put in a clothes dryer."

I stopped laughing. "I'm sorry," I said very seriously. "That wasn't nice of me. I've just never seen a dog smaller than I am, let alone one with your, um, rather unique features."

"I am pretty handsome, aren't I?" he stated. He looked at his reflection in the glass door he was standing by. "Very distinguished in fact. Just between you and me," he walked over to the fence to whisper to me, "the girls all go crazy over me."

Another point that proves just how kooky dogs are, I thought to myself. "My name's Charlie," I said to change the subject. "What's yours?"

"Pedro Jose Manuel Herrera Garcia the third. But you can call me Pepe."

I think my eyes crossed. "Why is your name so long?" I asked in fascination.

"I'm a show dog. They always give show dogs big fancy names. Couldn't you tell, just by lookin', that I am a very special dog?"

"Oh, yeah. I could tell from the first minute I saw you that you were really something different."

Just then the back door of Pepe's house opened. "Gotta go now Charlie, it's taco time!" He disappeared inside the house.

The thought of dinner made me realized I hadn't eaten in a while, so I went to the back door and meowed to get in. Amanda opened the door, and I wandered to the new kitchen to see where my food dish had been put.

The kitchen was covered in boxes. Mom was busy trying to unpack some pots and put them under the stove. I went over and rubbed up against her to get her attention.

"Hi Charlie," she said with a grin. "What do you think of our new home so far?"

"Meow." I said it in a rather non-committal voice.

I wasn't going to let them think I was happy just yet. I had a feeling I could use a sympathy angle to get some extra attention until they felt I had settled in. "Meow?"

"Oh, is it time for food already? I guess you really haven't eaten much since we got here." She opened a box and pulled out a bowl. Then she opened another box and dug around for awhile until she found the box of cat food and pulled it out. "Here you go," she said as she put the bowl on the floor. "Stick around Charlie. The rest of us are having pizza for dinner, and I imagine you'll get some of the goodies off Andrew's piece if you're under the table." Oh yeah! I do love pizza!

That first night in the new house was strange. Everyone was exhausted from the drive and unpacking, so they fell asleep right away. But not me. I was tired too, but as I laid there on Amanda's bed, I kept hearing all these strange noises. Most of them were just normal noises that a house makes, but since it was a different house, they were different noises. And from somewhere way off in the distance, I could hear a howling. It kind of sounded like a dog, but different. It was a haunting sound, and I felt as if it was a warning of things to come.

Chapter 7

Just Because I Do Something Stupid, That Doesn't Make Me A Dog

THE NEXT DAY WAS FILLED WITH unpacking activities. There were boxes all over the house, and Mom and Dad set to the task of putting everything away. Of course, half the time they couldn't remember where they had put things once they unpacked them, so whenever anyone wanted something, they had to either search boxes or cabinets, after asking everyone else if the item had been unpacked.

I had a lot of fun during that time. You see, as the boxes were emptied, Mom and Dad would stack them up in the front room. So there was this huge pile of empty boxes all stacked up and ready to climb. It was a feast for my active imagination. I never knew where I was going to land when I jumped up there. Sometimes I would land on top of a box and just sit there surveying the new house like a mountain lion. Sometimes the box would open, and I would be deep in a cave, hiding from a mysterious stalker. Sometimes I would land, the pile would rock sideways, and I would tumble to the ground in a great crashing of the box pile. That was a lot of fun, but then Dad would come and chase me away from the boxes so he could stack them back up. But as soon as he left the room again, boing! I jumped right back up on those boxes.

After a couple of hours, Dad got tired of chasing me away from the boxes and threw me out the back door. I landed on my paws, as always, and decided to spend a little more time exploring the back yard.

I was very careful to check over each plant before I sniffed it. It was surprising how many beautiful plants had nasty thorns all over them. It seemed like everything here had some kind of natural weapon. Even the trees had thorns on their branches. It gave me a strange kind of warning that I had better be careful. There must be a reason the plants are all armed, I thought to myself.

On the far side of the back yard was that big metal circle I had seen before. I didn't know what that could possibly be, so I went over to find out.

The metal sides were about four foot high. They went straight up, then had a little ledge on the very top. I was kind of nervous. Metal is tricky for cats to land on, we don't even like to walk on it because you can't grip it with your claws. The edge looked wide enough to stand on, and I really wanted to figure out what was inside this thing, but if I were to slip...

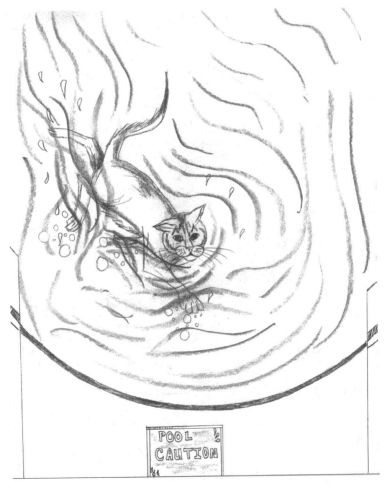

POOL ½
CAUTION

Buck up, Charlie, I told myself. You've never been

a wimp about things like this before. It's not like there's a vicious dog in there, you'd be able to smell it! What could possibly be dangerous inside a big circle? I jumped up to find out.

I landed on the top ledge, just barely. It wasn't very wide, only about three inches. Normally that wouldn't have been a problem. The problem was, the ledge was wet, and it sloped slightly inward, so my paws slipped on the water and I felt myself falling sideways.

I landed with a splash. This circle was a huge, cold, bathtub! I did my best cat-paddle, and was barely able to keep my head above water. Oh, this was worse than any bath I had ever taken. And the water smelled funny too. Like the bleach Mom used on Andrew's diapers when he was a baby. I swam to the edge, but the sides were smooth, and I just couldn't get a grip to hold on. I started meowing my head off, but I knew there was no one else in the back yard...

Then I heard her. There was one person outside that I had forgotten about. Frisky had been sleeping on the side of the house, but when she heard my cries for help she started barking her head off.

I heard the back door open. Mom was yelling out the door for Frisky to be quiet, but when Frisky just barked louder, Mom came to see what the problem was. I saw the look of horror on her face as she saw me swimming around the pool. She reached down and pulled me out.

I was shivering so hard against Mom's chest that my whole body was shaking like an earthquake. I was freezing cold, and I was very scared. I had swallowed a bunch of water, so my stomach was rolling like the tide. Mom took me inside and went straight to the bathroom to grab a towel. Luckily they were unpacked already and she found one right away. As she walked through the house she called out to the rest of the family. They all came running, and each one reached over to comfort me as she told them what had happened.

Mom sat in a chair and pulled me down onto her lap, the towel still wrapped around me. She rubbed me all over with the soft material, and some of my shivers went away. Dad turned the heater on, and when Mom had squeezed all the water out of my fur that she could, she set me on a dry towel by the heating duct.

I was still soaking wet, and shivering like crazy. The hot air from the vent felt really good, and I was just starting to relax when Amanda and Andrew burst out laughing.

"Charlie looks so funny all soaking wet and shaking!" Amanda giggled. "He looks like a Chihuahua!"

"Yeah! Wanna taco Chawlie?" Andrew joined in.

I looked down at myself. I was so wet, my fur was

stuck down to my sides just as if I didn't have any. My tail looked like an electric cord, it was so thin without the fur, and I could tell my ears and whiskers were sticking up like streetlights without my fur around them. I knew I didn't look good, but saying I looked like a dog? That really hurt!

"I think Charlie learned an important lesson today, and I want you both to learn it as well," Mom was saying. "The swimming pool is no place to horse around, or explore without a parent with you. New rule as of today, no one goes within three feet of the pool unless Dad or I are out back with you. Understood?"

"Yes," Andrew said.

"You got it Mom," Amanda piped in.

"Meow," I added.

Chapter 8

Help! I'm Going Bald!

TIME WENT BY PRETTY QUICKLY THE NEXT FEW WEEKS. Amanda started going to a new school, which she really liked, and Andrew, Mom and I got into our new routine. Then, without any warning at all, the heat came.

The heat in Arizona is nothing like the heat in Northern California. It sneaks up and just starts, then never stops. In California, the heat would build up. Each day might get a little hotter, but then it would cool down each night. In Arizona, it just kept building up.

I didn't notice it too much at first. I just changed my routine and only went into the back yard early in the morning and late in the afternoon. Then I woke up one morning and knew something was different.

I wasn't sure what it was at first. I felt lighter, like I had lost weight. I also felt a little itchy, so I reached up with my back leg to scratch my side. When my rear paw pulled back, it was full of fur.

I looked down at myself. As I raised up off of Amanda's bed where I had been sleeping, I saw hundreds of hairs that had fallen off during the night. Well, maybe not hundreds, but it seemed like it! I let out a confused cry.

"What's the matter, Charlie?" Amanda opened her eyes and reached down to pet me. When her hand came away, it had fur all over it, and a cloud of fur puffed out into the air around us.

Amanda rubbed her nose as the fur started tickling her. "Oh Charlie, you're shedding like crazy!" she said as she pushed me off the bed.

I looked up at her as she sat on the bed, waving the cloud of fur away from her face. Like it's my fault! I'm losing all my fur, and she's mad at me?

I left the room in a huff and went to find Mom. Maybe she could help me. I needed help, and I knew it. I mean, I had shed before. All cats do, and it's a natural process. But this wasn't like normal shedding. It seemed like all my hair was coming out at once!

The moment I walked into the kitchen, it hit me again. That terrible itch. I stopped just inside the doorway, reached up my back paw, and started scratching with a vengeance. I was surrounded within seconds by a cloud of fur.

Mom looked up. "Charlie? Oh my goodness!"

Good ol' Mom. I could always depend on her. She was the one who fed me, watched over me, took such good care of me, why she even saved me from the pool! I knew she would have some sympathy for my situation and would take care of the problem.

"Oh Charlie! You're getting fur all over the food!" She picked me up and dumped me out the back door.

Well, so much for all that stuff about mothers being so nurturing.

It was later in the day than I was used to getting up, so I wasn't ready for how hot it was outside. I started sweating immediately, and that just made the loose fur stick to me and itch even more. I sat there on the porch, trying to hide from the sun, scratching like crazy, until I heard a voice from up on the wall.

"Hey, Charlie!" It was Blackie. "I see you've got the springtime sheds!"

"The what?" I asked.

"The springtime sheds. It happens to everyone here. The heat hits, and all of a sudden, whoosh! All your fur seems to come out at once. But don't worry about it. Just enough fur stays on to keep you from being naked, but not so much that you're miserable all summer."

"That's good to hear. I thought I was going bald," I said as another huge puff of fur flew up from me. "Man, it's really hot out here. How much longer does summer last?"

Blackie started laughing so hard I thought he would fall off the fence. "Summer? Charlie, it's only April. Summer isn't for two more months yet. This is only spring. In the summer, you won't see any animals outside when the sun is up. Night time is the only time to be outside during the summer, and even then it's way too hot." A voice sounded from the other side of the fence. "Uh-oh, that's Ralph, our dog, calling. Must be time for breakfast. I'll catch you later Charlie," and he disappeared over the side of the fence.

I spent the next few minutes scratching off and pushing away from me as much of the loose hair as I could. It took a while, but finally I could get up and walk around without a fog of fur surrounding me. I walked over to where Frisky was sleeping in the shade in a corner of the yard. She had actually dug a small hole in the dirt, so she wouldn't be so hot. It did look nice and cool, but too messy for my taste.

Out of the corner of my eye I saw some movement. It was under a short green bush with yellow flowers. I had explored that plant before, so I knew there were no thorns to worry about. Finally, something good was going to happen this morning! My first chance at bug hunting since we moved.

I crept slowly toward the bush, keeping my eyes focused on where I had seen the movement. It had been near the edge of the plant, so the bug was either on his way in, or on his way out. If he was coming out, I wanted to be ready for him.

I froze when I saw the movement again. I didn't know what kind of bug this was. If it was fast, or able to jump, I didn't want it to know I was there until it was too late. It came out of the bush slowly. It was unlike any bug I had ever seen before. It was long and thin, with four legs on each side, plus a pincher like a crab on each side of its head. It had beady little eyes that I could hardly see, and a long tail that curled up over it's long body and rested over it's back. This was one weird bug! And I wanted to see if he tasted as strange as he looked.

I continued to watch as it slowly made it's way across the yard. It didn't move very fast, and those legs didn't look like jumpers, so I decided to creep a little closer for a better look.

As I approached the bug, it either didn't see me or wasn't concerned about me, I wasn't sure which, but it just kept up it's slow walk across the yard. I got up right behind it and gave it a little push, just to see what would happen.

The bug spun around and looked at me. It waved it's tail around, and I noticed a little sharp point like a bee's stinger on that tail. I knew about bee's. I had taken a bite of one of those once. Once. So I was cautious as I stuck out my paw to give the bug another whack.

This bug surprised me. Most creatures that are smaller than us either run or play dead when a cat messes with them. This guy seemed like he was just itching for a fight, and was ready to take me on, even though he was only about one and one-half inches long.

I was just about ready to go in for kill when I heard Dad at the back door. He had come out calling for Frisky, but when he saw me crouched in the corner he came my direction.

"What have you got there, Charlie?" He came right up next to me. I hadn't moved, because I didn't want this bug to get away. Dad had asked me in the past what I was hunting, and he was usually happy to see me chasing off insects. But this time, instead of letting me continue the hunt, I saw his big shoe land on the bug, squishing it.

I looked up at him, my disappointment written on my face.

"Charlie," Dad reached down and picked me up, "trust me. You don't want to mess with scorpions."

He carried me into the house, then told Mom we needed to call an exterminator and not to let the kids or me out back without supervision until they had taken care of the scorpion problem. Mom looked really disturbed at the prospect of these weird bugs. I figured it was because they were so funky looking, but then I heard Dad telling Amanda and Andrew all about them, and why they should avoid them. It seems these little bugs have some really bad poison in those stingers of theirs. Some can just make you hurt, some can make you really sick, and some can even kill you.

Blackie had been right, anything and everything around here could be dangerous. I really should have paid closer attention to that. But I still hadn't totally learned that lesson.

Chapter 9

A Walk On The Wild Side

IT WAS HOT. It was so hot. Too hot to play. Too hot to eat. Too hot to move, so I just laid there on the tile floor waiting for it to cool down. I had been waiting for over a month.

The days had taken on a familiar pattern. I would wake up in the morning, stretch, use the litter box, and make my way to the kitchen. Amanda was out of school for the summer, so I let her sleep. Mom was usually up, doing housework, because it would be too hot later in the day to get anything physical done. I would rub up against her legs and meow good morning.

"Good morning to you Charlie. You want some milk?" she would ask.

Mom used to offer me warm milk every morning, but she had stopped heating it lately. I guess she realized the last thing I wanted was something warm.

I would have my milk, eat some breakfast, and find someplace cool to lay down for the day. Just eating seemed to get me over-heated. Over the course of the summer I had worked on developing interesting sleeping places to relax in during the heat of the day. The tile floor in the entry was a favorite. The bathtub. The smooth top of the dining room table was comfortable, but Mom always yelled at me if she caught me there. The sink in the bathroom was nice and cool, but sometimes people would get irritated when they wanted to wash their hands and I was in the way. If I didn't move fast enough, they'd occasionally turn the water on with me still in there. And you know how I hate getting wet.

The heat was getting to everybody. Dad went to work each day, so he got out of the house. But it was too hot for the kids to play outside unless they were swimming, so they played indoors all day. That made them rowdy and Mom crazy.

In fact, Mom began to go so nuts about the weather that she wrote a poem about it. It went like this:

An Arizona Mother's Prayer
Thank you Lord for another beautiful sunny day.
Thank you for air conditioning.

Thank you for the beautiful flowers that bloom here all year, they look pretty through the windows. I'd love to go smell them, but it's too hot.

Thank you that it was only 118° today. It was 120° yesterday, and they predict 122° tomorrow, thanks for the short break.

Thank you Lord for air conditioning.

Please send angels to watch over my children's feet so they won't trip and fall, you can get third degree burns from the sidewalk.

Thank you Lord for shoes.

Thank you Lord for swimming pools.

Thank you for indoor malls.

Thank you for VCR's, Walt Disney and his movies.

Thank you for cars, so we can drive to the mountains on weekends to escape the heat for a few hours.

Thank you for making summer only 3 months long.

Thank you Lord for air conditioning.

I had been in the house all day. It had been too hot to be outside with a fur coat on. And mine's not removable.

The rest of the family had been outside. They had played in the pool for hours. Fine for them. Splashing and frolicking in the water. Yuck. I had nothing to do but lie inside near an air conditioning vent to try to stay cool.

I was bored.

When it got dark outside I decided it was time to do something. If I couldn't get out during the day to explore the neighborhood, I'd do it at night. I went to the back door, meowed, and was let out.

"Don't go too far, Charlie," I heard Mom say as I walked out. "It's getting late."

What did I care what time it was. Cats don't wear watches. I'd been sleeping all day, and it was going to be just as hot tomorrow, so I'd be sleeping most of the day again. So tonight was my only time to be out and about. Besides, I had always heard that night-time was when cats could really howl. And I was ready to HOWWWWLLLLL........

I jumped up on the garbage cans, onto the fence, and walked around to where I could jump into the front yard. I hadn't got a chance to explore the neigh-borhood farther than Blackie's and Pepe's houses, so I wanted to see what there was to see.

I jumped down from the fence onto the sidewalk. OW! OH! OUCH! EW! The sidewalk was burning hot! Each one of my paws burned with every step. As I ran for the grass, I could only imagine how funny I looked. I was arched up, running my fastest and trying not to touch the ground with any of my paws. Only one paw was touching the ground at any time, the other three were way up against my body. I must have looked like a wobbling bowling ball with a peg sticking out of the bottom.

When I reached the grass I looked around until I saw a small puddle of water near a leaking sprinkler. I went over and put my paws in one by one to cool them down. Ahh....I swear I could see steam rising from them.

I rested for a moment and considered my problem. It had been so hot all day that the sidewalk had absorbed the heat and hadn't cooled down yet. I would have to travel slowly, cutting through front yards and running across short stretches of cement only when necessary.

I looked at each house as I walked by on my way down the street. I didn't take to time to explore each one closely, I would do that later. Right now I just wanted to get a feel of the area. The lay of the land, you know?

As I approached the end of the street I could smell sweet flowers. The farther I went, the stronger the scent got until it was almost overwhelming. When I got to the corner I could see what it was.

There was a huge field of trees. It looked like hundreds of them! They were covered in green leaves, white flowers, and yellow fruit. It was a lemon orchard!

The ground around the trees was all big clumps of dirt. I imagined the farmer who owned the land must have chopped it up with some kind of tractor or something to keep the weeds from taking over. I had to walk very slowly and carefully because my paws were still tender from the burning sidewalk, and the dirt clods were dry and sharp and they kind of hurt to step on. As I walked, I tried to picture a tractor little enough to fit under the branches of the trees and how the farmer would have to bend over to keep from getting whacked in the face. Then I began to picture myself driving the tractor. Can't you just see me, my front paws on the wheel, a stalk of hay in my mouth, humming 'Old MacDonald' while driving my 'John Deer'?

I was so busy driving the fields in my mind that I didn't notice how far I was wandering into the orchard. I suddenly realized I had walked so deep into the trees that I could no longer see or hear the street behind me.

But I could hear something. I stopped and looked all around, but I couldn't see anything. I turned around and started heading back the way I had come.

From behind a large tree in front of me, a dog jumped out. At least, I thought it was a dog. It was big, a little bigger than Frisky, but very thin. It's fur was long and wiry, and looked like it had never been brushed. Or washed. It smelled awful. It's ears were long and pointed, and so was it's nose. It's mouth was slightly open, and drool was dripping from it's long, sharp teeth.

"I reckon it must be dinner time," said a deep voice as a smile broke across his face.

I misunderstood. "Mine was hours ago. If I had any left I'd share it with you, but I was really hungry and ate it all."

"Well that's just dandy. It means you alls well fed, plump and juicy."

I hadn't had a dog threaten to eat me since I was a kitten. "Look," I said, trying not to appear scared. "I have a couple of friends who are dogs, and I know that they really don't like to eat cats. Chase us, yes. Eat us, no."

"Well, I reckon that's so, but I ain't no dog."

"You ain't? I mean, you're not?" my voice was beginning to quiver.

"Nope. I'm a coyote, and we definitely does eat cats."

He lunged at me then, and I leaped to the trunk of the nearest tree and started climbing. I scrambled past branches, going higher and higher, until I couldn't go any further. Then I stopped to look down. The coyote had his front paws on the trunk of the tree, and I could see his long toe nails. He was stretching up off the ground to reach as far as he could. He was pretty tall, all stretched out like that, and since it wasn't a very big tree, he could reach up fairly high. Luckily, not quite high enough.

"You shor is fast fer a house cat," he complained. "But ya cain't stay up there ferever."

Given the alternative, spending my life on a branch didn't sound too bad. Then an idea hit me. "Who are you calling a house cat?" I hissed, as if the thought was outrageous. "I happen to be a baby cougar."

"Huh?" he said, looking me over very carefully in the semi-darkness. "Yer color is right, but we ain't had no cougars 'round here fer a long time."

"Well...me and my mom, we just moved down here. Yeah. You see...," I was trying to think fast, "the hunting was getting bad near our old home, so we had to look for a new place. So, you better back off and get out of here before my mom comes back, or you're the one who'll be dinner."

He jumped down and started circling the tree, watching me. Then he stopped and reached up the trunk again, trying to get a better look. "I don't believes you," he finally said. "You may have cougar lookin' fur, but you got a kitty cat face."

"You better not let my mom hear you say that," I cried. This deception was my only hope, so I continued to play it out, even though it wasn't working. "She hears you say a thing like that and she'll start eating you before you're even dead. How would you like that, huh? I bet she'd even let me eat your ears, and that's the tastiest part of a coyote." I thought that was a great line, especially since I had never heard of a coyote before that day.

He looked a little shook-up for a moment, then the mean gleam came back into his eyes. "All right, if'n you're a cougar, then you call yer ma right now."

Uh oh, this was it. He wouldn't believe me anymore once I called out and no one answered. "You're sure you want me to do that?" I asked.

"Go ahead."

"Okay. Mom, oh mother... where are you?"

From a few trees away, the screech of a wildcat met our ears. Then a long, low growl.

The coyote freaked out. His eyes just about popped out of his head, and he went running as fast as he could into the orchard. He was out of sight within seconds.

I was frozen. A coyote was bad enough, but at least they couldn't climb. A cougar could. And if I was about to meet one, face to face, I didn't think he would spare my life just because we were both members of the cat family.

I tried to see farther through the darkness as I heard footsteps coming from the direction where the screech had sounded. I blinked. I blinked again. Could it be? But how? "Blackie?" I asked.

"Hey Charlie. I think you can come down now. That coyote won't be back this way tonight."

"But what about the cougar?" I was still peering into the darkness.

Blackie laughed. "That was me. I saw you wander into the orchard and followed you to make sure you didn't run into any trouble. I tried to warn you about the dangers of the desert. When I saw that mangy scavenger go after you I was afraid I was too late. But I hid out and waited, and when I heard that cougar line you were feeding him, I just played along."

I climbed down the tree and jumped to land next to Blackie. "Thank you so much! Wow, you were great! You had me scared to death! How did you ever learn to screech and growl like that?"

"Singing the blues, Charlie, singing the blues." We began to walk back toward the street.

"What were you doing out on the streets tonight Charlie? I don't remember seeing you out of your own yard before."

"I haven't been. I was just going so crazy being stuck inside because of the heat, that I wanted to get out and get some excitement."

"Was that exciting enough for you?" Blackie laughed. "You got a lot to learn my young friend." He looked thoughtful for a moment. Then he smiled. "You want some excitement? I'll show you excitement, cat style."

Chapter 10

The Jazz Singer

I FOLLOWED BLACKIE OUT OF THE ORCHARD, but when we got to the street he didn't head toward home.

"Where are we going?" I asked. I didn't want to wander too far. I'd had a good scare and didn't think my system could handle the terror of being lost. Been there. Done that.

"Trust me Charlie. We're not going far, and you're gonna love this."

He was right, we didn't have to go very far. After only half a block, we jumped over a low fence and into a back yard. Blackie headed toward the hedge that lined the back fence and signaled for me to follow as he slipped through a small opening in the branches. I followed him slowly, not really knowing what to expect.

"Wow! This is awesome!" I wasn't sure if I said that out loud or not, I was too busy staring at my surroundings. The hedge wasn't against the back fence as I had thought. There was a big space in between, so that it created an enclosed area surrounded on three sides by fences, and the other side by the hedge. Inside this space the neighborhood cats had created quite a nightclub. There were several flower pots, turned upside down, that served as tables. There were two crates turned over down at one end that served as the stage. On the stage itself was a kid's toy piano, a miniature drum set, and a tiny trombone, all being played by cats. Surprisingly, they sounded really good! I wasn't very familiar with jazz, having been raised with mostly classical music, but it had a great beat and a smooth sound.

There were several cats sitting around at the makeshift tables. Some had brought 'picnics' with them; cat food, small rodents, and an occasional bug were scattered on the various tables. Everyone was watching the stage intently, most either bobbing their heads or swinging their tails to the beat. When the band finished the song they were playing, a chorus of meows went up in applause.

"Let me introduce you to some of the gang," Blackie said, and he started walking to one of the tables in the back of the 'club'. But before he got a chance to get the attention of the cats at that table, the piano player noticed him.

"Well, take a look at who finally showed up everybody. It's Blackie! Come on up here and give us a song Blackie!" he called out.

Blackie started to shake his head and signal that he would be up in a minute, when the entire audience started chanting. "Blackie, Blackie, Blackie!"

Blackie smiled at me and headed up toward the stage. I just stood where I was, figuring I would watch him perform from the back of the room. Wrong.

"Well, a very fine evening to each and every one of you," Blackie said as he stepped up on stage. "I was just about to introduce a new member of the neighborhood to a few cats, but I guess it will just be easier to let you meet him all at once, and make him take the official 'Kitt-Catt Club' initiation. Come on up here Charlie!"

I froze. He signaled again for me to come up. I just stood there, with my mouth forming a small 'o' in shock, and one paw on my chest as if to say "Who, me?"

"Come on Charlie, we don't bite. At least, not usually." The crowd laughed at that one. I felt someone come up behind and start pushing me toward the stage.

Okay, I told myself. Nothing to be afraid of. You can handle this. After all, he's just going to introduce you, and then you can sit down. With these words of encouragement ringing inside my head, I stepped up on stage.

"Everybody, this is Charlie. Make sure you come up to him later and introduce yourselves. Charlie just moved here a few months ago, and this is his first night out.

Let's make it a great one!" Everyone cheered a welcome to me at Blackie's speech. I smiled. Maybe this would be all right.

Then that hope was trashed for good. "And now everyone," Blackie continued, "Charlie will sing us his first song." He started to walk off the stage.

I grabbed him. "What do you mean, I'll sing a song?" I hissed in his ear. "I don't sing!"

"Every cat knows how to sing Charlie. Just let that natural talent in you shine through. You'll do great." With that, he left the stage.

I stood there, staring at the audience. I'd never tried to sing, let alone for a bunch of cats I didn't even know. I tried to think of a song, but nothing came to me. Then I remembered my upbringing. After all, I grew up surrounded with classical music, there was no reason I couldn't use one of those songs. But what was appropriate, that I could actually sing?

Beethoven. Always my favorite. But which symphony? The natural choice was Beethoven's Fifth, as it had such a catchy tune.

So I began. "Meow meow meow meeow...meow meow meow meeow..."

The cats sitting in front of me looked stunned. Blackie rushed up on stage and stopped me. "Was I that bad?" I asked him.

"No Charlie, your voice was fine, but this is a blues

club. You've got to sing the blues."

"But I don't know any blues songs," I said. This wasn't good. How was I going to make friends with the neighbors if I walked off the stage a failure?

"Everyone has the blues inside them Charlie, you just have to learn how to let it out. Hey everybody, how about if I help Charlie get started, would that be all right?"

The cats all cheered, and Blackie signaled for the band to start playing. His song started like this:

> My old man is sick,
> my lady's at the mall,
> my girl is at school,
> and the baby's too small,
> I got the low down,
> no one's changed my litter box blues, oh yeah!
> I got those low low down, no one's changed
> my litter box blues, uh huh.

He leaned over to me. "Now you take it Charlie."

I stepped to the edge of the stage and, in the same rhythm and tune that Blackie had used, I made up my own words to the song:

> The box is so full,
> I don't want to dig,
> And as for the smell,
> well the stinks gettin' big!
> I got the low down,
> no one's changed my litter box blues, oh yeah!

I got those low low low down, no one's
changed my litter box blues, uh huh.
I can't use my box,
don't want to use the floor,
so I'm standing here screaming:
Let me out the back door!
I got the low down,
no one's changed my litter box blues, oh yeah!
I got those low low low down, no one's
changed my litter box blues, uh huh.

The crowd went wild. The clapping went on for several minutes, as Blackie patted me on the back and told me to take a bow. Wow! I had never felt anything like that before. It was the coolest thing that had ever happened to me.

When I stepped off the stage several cats came up and introduced themselves. I was invited over to table after table where other cats shared their food and told me about themselves and their families. I shared stories of my family and even explained about my misadventure with the coyote earlier that night.

Blackie and the band played on, singing late into the night until we started to see the sun peaking its head above the edge of the mountains. I couldn't believe it! I had been out all night! Everyone started leaving then, and the band called it quits and went home to sleep. Blackie came over to me and we walked back home together.

"Wow, what a night! It's hard to believe so much could happen to me in such a short time," I said. "I want to thank you for saving my life last night, and for introducing me to such wonderful friends. I had a great time."

"Just let me know when you want to do it again, Charlie. You're welcome to sing with us anytime you wish. You have a great voice, and I have a feeling you have a talent for the blues."

I blushed at his compliment. Luckily, you can't see a cat's skin turn pink through all the fur.

When we reached my house, Blackie waved good-bye and said he would see me soon. Feeling too tired to jump the fence, I went up to the front door and meowed.

Mom opened the door within a few seconds. She looked at me as she opened the door, and I knew I was in trouble.

"I hope you had a good time out there. I was worried sick about you. Don't you know what can happen to a little cat out there in the middle of the night?"

I do now. "Meow," I said, trying to sound as sorry as possible.

"Yeah, a likely excuse. Now go on in, get some food and water and get to sleep. You must be exhausted." She had no idea.

After a small bite and some water, I went into Amanda's room and collapsed on the bed. I think I was asleep before my fur even hit the pillow.

Chapter 11

Puppy Love

I SLEPT FOR SEVERAL HOURS. By the time I woke up, Mom was making lunch.

"Good morning Lazy-bones," Amanda said to me.

"Meow," I answered. I went over to where she was sitting at the table and rubbed against her legs. I was rewarded with some turkey from her sandwich.

I ate some of my own food, then went out back to see what kind of a day it was. Still hot.

I noticed Frisky was standing next to the fence by Pepe's yard. Actually, she wasn't standing but leaning against the fence. Her expression looked even more vacant than usual, if that's possible.

I walked over to her. She was sighing, over and over again. Sigh. Sigh.

"What's with you?" I asked her.

"I'm in love!" she said in that dizzy voice of hers,

and sighed again.

I looked around the yard. "With who," I asked, "the lizards?"

"With Pepe," she said dreamily. "I can just picture him. He's big and strong, with a short muzzle, floppy ears, and big brown eyes. I'll bet he has long legs with big muscles, and a tail that sticks straight out behind him." She sighed again.

I jumped up on top of the fence and looked over. Pepe was leaning against his side of the fence, wearing the same dopey expression that Frisky had.

"What's up Pepe?" I asked.

"I'm in love man," he answered. "I can just imagine her. She's a little angel, small and intelligent with bulgy black eyes and a curly little tail." Then he sighed.

I looked at Frisky, the Labrador.

I looked at Pepe, the Chihuahua.

"Am I right about him?" Frisky asked.

"Am I right about her?" Pepe asked.

I thought about it a moment. They would be heartbroken if they knew the truth about each other. If I wasn't there, they would never have had anyone to tell them they were wrong. And since they would probably never meet face to face, they could continue to happily love each other without their looks getting in the way.

So I took myself out of the picture. "Yeah, right," I

said, without letting them know if it was a straight answer or sarcasm.

I jumped down on our side of the fence. Frisky sighed again and said, "Isn't Arizona great?"

Yeah, right.

On my way back to the door, I caught a new kind of bug that I had never seen before. I don't know what it was. It looked kind of like a skinny grasshopper, but it said its prayers before I ate it. Very tasty.

I went back inside. A few minutes later, Amanda came flying through the front door. She picked me up in her arms and swung me around in circles (I was good at holding on by now).

"Oh Charlie, Maria just told me I was her very best friend, and she's inviting me to sleep over and go swimming in her huge pool! I have a best friend again! Isn't Arizona great?"

Yeah, right. It's getting there.

That evening, the whole family was gathered out back. They were playing this game with rackets, trying to hit this little plastic thing over a net they had put up. They called the plastic thing a birdie, but they didn't fool me. I took a close look at it and it didn't look anything like bird. It didn't taste like one either.

Suddenly Mom stopped playing. She was just staring at the sky. "Wow," I heard her say. "Take a look at that." We all looked up.

The sky was turning the most amazing colors. I had watched sunsets in California and they were really pretty, but this was awesome. The sky turned colors I didn't even know existed; neon pinks, purples, gold and this incredible rose. There was a storm brewing in the distance, and the sunset was framed in dark purple with lightning streaking down.

Wow.

Blackie jumped up on the fence just then. "Hey Charlie, you were a big hit last night. You coming by the club tonight?" When I continued to stare at the sky without answering, he turned to see what we were looking at. "Takes your breath away, doesn't it?" he said. "The sky here puts on shows that TV can only dream of matching. Isn't Arizona wonderful?"

Yeah, right, I thought. Only this time, I meant it.